SASHA AND THE DRAGON

by Laura E. Wolfe

Illustrated by Nicholas Malara

ANCIENT FAITH
PUBLISHING

CHESTERTON, INDIANA

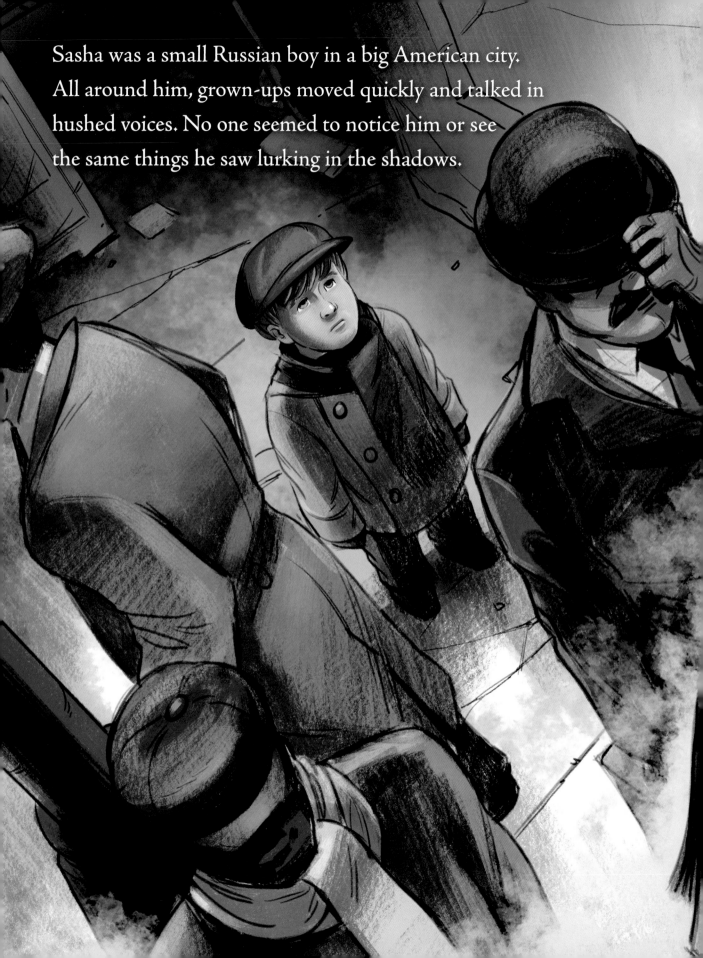

Sasha was a small Russian boy in a big American city. All around him, grown-ups moved quickly and talked in hushed voices. No one seemed to notice him or see the same things he saw lurking in the shadows.

Down the hall, his old Baba lay
in a bedroom that smelled like the
dead crow he had found at the park.
She didn't sing to him anymore.

*Sasha was afraid
of that room.*

A cluster of children from the other apartments laughed and pointed when he walked by. They said his name as if a joke was hidden in it somewhere. Instead of the kind glances of friends, he felt daggers of ice in their gazes.

Sasha was afraid of
the other children.

When his mother took him for walks on the concrete, he longed for the wide, wild spaces surrounding his old village near the river. The sky was so small here; he wondered how all the clouds could squeeze in and still leave room for the sun to nourish the green, growing things.

*Sasha was afraid
of the city.*

But at night, when Sasha lay in his bed, staring at the streetlight outside his window, he was the most afraid of all. He trembled because he knew that dragons skulked here in this new land,

monsters of gloom and loneliness that had never heard of
warrior saints or special signs to drive away the evil one. He
blessed himself with the sign of the cross, but still he was miserable.

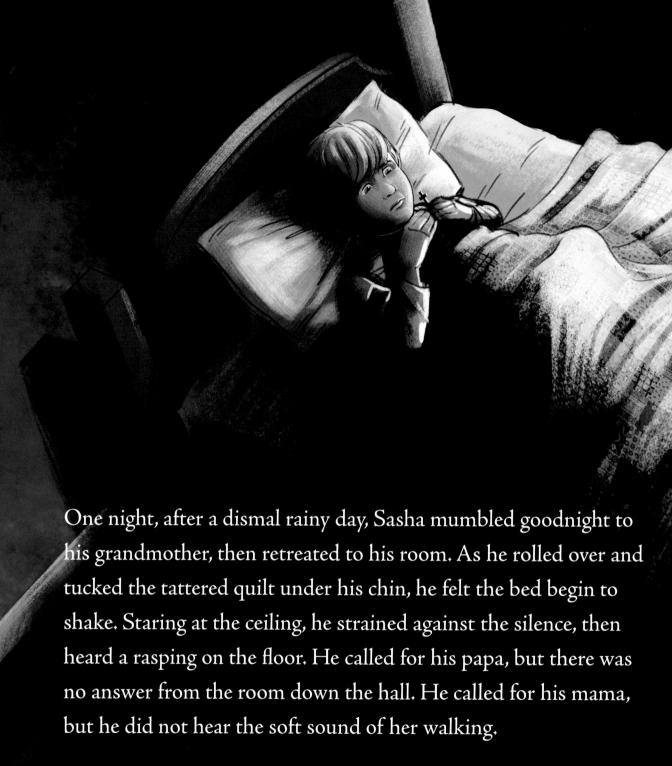

One night, after a dismal rainy day, Sasha mumbled goodnight to his grandmother, then retreated to his room. As he rolled over and tucked the tattered quilt under his chin, he felt the bed begin to shake. Staring at the ceiling, he strained against the silence, then heard a rasping on the floor. He called for his papa, but there was no answer from the room down the hall. He called for his mama, but he did not hear the soft sound of her walking.

He screwed his eyes shut, then kissed the wooden cross that hung around his neck.

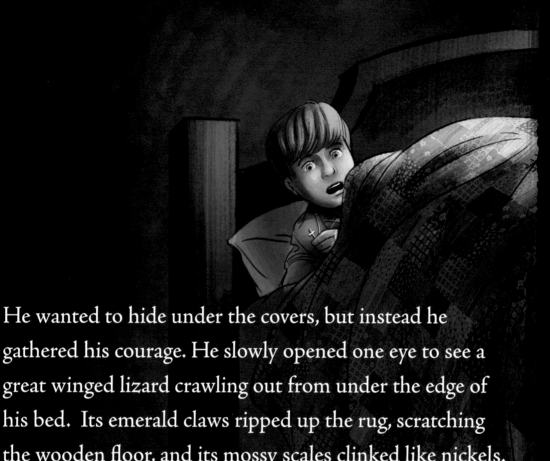

He wanted to hide under the covers, but instead he
gathered his courage. He slowly opened one eye to see a
great winged lizard crawling out from under the edge of
his bed. Its emerald claws ripped up the rug, scratching
the wooden floor, and its mossy scales clinked like nickels.
Its forked tongue tested the air, a black feather poking
out the side of its mouth. A cloud of murk filled the
space around its leathery wings.

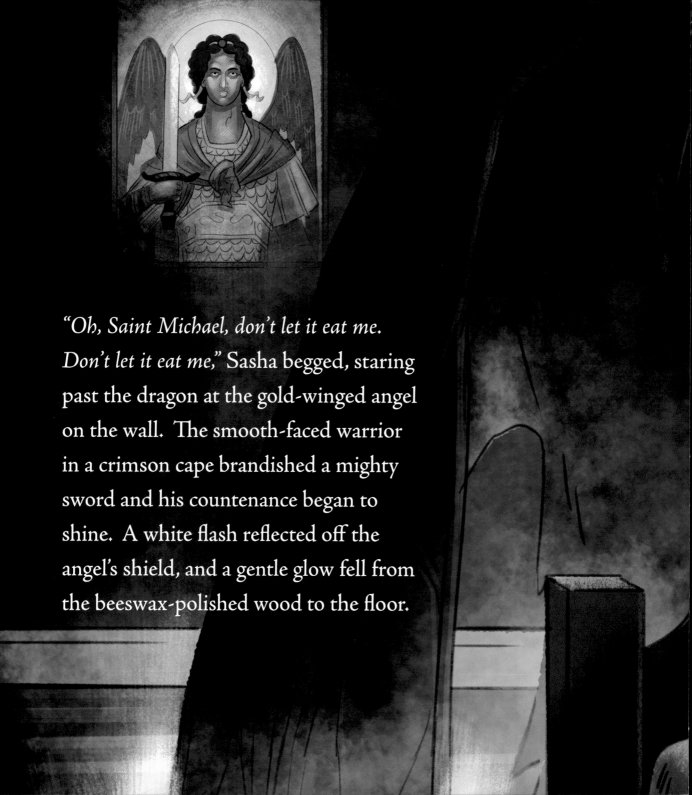

"*Oh, Saint Michael, don't let it eat me. Don't let it eat me,*" Sasha begged, staring past the dragon at the gold-winged angel on the wall. The smooth-faced warrior in a crimson cape brandished a mighty sword and his countenance began to shine. A white flash reflected off the angel's shield, and a gentle glow fell from the beeswax-polished wood to the floor.

The serpent slid over the footboard, its nails catching in the quilt, pulling it to the floor. Sasha could smell the dragon's mildew breath, and though he squirmed up against the headboard, the beast inched closer. Sasha's heart knocked painfully against his ribs and his vision tunneled, narrowing in on Saint Michael's blade.

"Kill it with your sword!"

He scrambled to his knees
and pointed at the beast.

"Kill it with your sword!"

Trumpets sounded in the distance, then clarion call drawing closer and growing louder with every second. The air filled with the scent of incense and ozone. A crack like lightning split the room, and the archangel Michael charged his scarlet steed out of the icon.

The magnificent guardian swung his great sword, and the blade carving the air sounded like glory. The dragon shattered into a million mirror shards, and the angel's gilded wings beat a blast of victory. A warm wind rushed around the room, tasting like summer and ringing like church bells.

When Sasha awoke the next morning, wrapped snugly in his quilt, he discovered a gold-tipped feather lying across a gouge in the floor. Outside, cars honked in the city streets and hurried people bustled like angry geese, but inside the apartment, everything was calm. Morning light filled the room, like the glow of Saint Michael's face.

Sasha carefully lifted the feather
from the floor and held it up to the
sunshine. He breathed in deeply,
savoring its holy scent. Then he tucked
it into his cap and dressed. Today,

Sasha was not afraid.

After breakfast, he went for a walk in the city with his mother.
Sunlight glittered on glass and chrome, illuminating corners that
had previously seemed shadowed. He lingered in the park, listening
to birds sing in the newly blossoming trees. As he watched,
a shed ruby feather drifted softly through the air and landed
at his feet. He held it up next to the golden feather, marveling
at their shared beauty. Truly God and His angels were close,
wrapping peace around his heart.

Outside his building, he passed a neighbor boy who snickered and whispered in his brother's ear. Sasha took the red feather from his pocket and offered it to the boy, who gaped in puzzlement as he received it.

When he returned home, Sasha walked reverently down the hall to his Baba's room. She was asleep when he went in, but he kissed her on the cheek and climbed up to sit next to her.

"Don't be afraid, Baba," he said, placing the angelic feather in her open hand. Baba opened her eyes and smiled, slowly closing her fingers around Sasha's. Then, with the joyous words of Baba's old song,

Sasha began to sing.

MORE ABOUT
SAINT MICHAEL AND HIS ICONS

Stories about Saint Michael in the Old Testament tell us that he is the chief commander of the heavenly armies. That's why his icons often show him prepared for battle with a sword or a lance. He also carries what looks like a shield that bears a representation of Christ: an "X" for "Xristos"; the Chi-Ro, the letters "ICXC," which means "Jesus Christ Conquers"; or a picture of Christ Himself. Technically, it's not a shield—it's an orb that represents Jesus Christ and His kingdom, and it shows us that Saint Michael has authority on earth.

Saint Michael also appears in an icon called "The Apocalypse," which tells us about the Second Coming of Christ according to the Revelation of Saint John. In this icon, Saint Michael is depicted blowing the trumpet of judgment, swinging a censer, and carrying the Gospel, all while riding a red winged horse. Some-

times he is also shown with a rainbow over his head, with a lance or a cross, and sometimes he is shown defeating a dragon. The color red is a symbol both of courage and of the victory of the resurrection, and wings symbolize swiftness to obey the will of God. All of these elements show us how Saint Michael is active in doing God's work on earth.

Saint Michael can also be found in many icons of Old Testament stories, such as protecting the Three Holy Youths in the fiery furnace, visiting Daniel in the lions' den, and announcing the Lord to Joshua. In church, Saint Michael and Saint Gabriel are depicted in icons with ribbons around their ears, showing their special spiritual hearing—they hear both the voice of God and our prayers. By their prayers, may we be listeners and warriors for God and His kingdom!

Saint Michael's primary feast day is the Synaxis of the Archangels on November 8.

TROPARION—TONE 4

Michael, commander of the heavenly hosts, / we who are unworthy beseech you, / by your prayers encompass us beneath the wings of your immaterial glory, / and faithfully preserve us who fall down and cry out to you: / "Deliver us from all harm, for you are the commander of the powers on high!"

SPECIAL THANKS TO
Father Stephen Freeman and James Freeman,
for sharing the truth of a child's prayer and inspiring this story.

AUTHOR & ILLUSTRATOR

LAURA E. WOLFE is a summa cum laude graduate of Kutztown University who lives and works in rural Pennsylvania. Her short stories and poetry can be found in *The Soul of Wit*, an anthology of subcreative fiction from Oloris Publishing. She and her family are members of St. Paul Antiochian Orthodox Church in Emmaus, Pennsylvania.

NICHOLAS MALARA grew up in Denver, Colorado, where he earned a Bachelor of Fine Arts degree in Illustration. He has been blessed with a career in professional art for over sixteen years. Since his conversion ten years ago, he has also been a student of Orthodox iconography. He currently resides in Spokane, Washington, with his wife and two children.

In loving memory of Tamara Lynn Teslovich Wolfe, my mom,
who told me I was strong until I believed her. —LEW

To my children Luca and Nina, who bring color to my life. —NM

Sasha and the Dragon
Text copyright © 2017 Laura E. Wolfe
Illustrations copyright © 2017 Nicholas Malara

Troparion of Saint Michael found at oca.org under The Lives of the Saints—September 6.
Archangel Michael Icon by Father Photios Cooper—https://www.flickr.com/photos/frphotios/.

Published by:
Ancient Faith Publishing
A division of Ancient Faith Ministries
PO Box 748
Chesterton, IN 46304

ISBN: 978-1-944967-27-7